BEYOND THE DREAM

ALAN CIPHER

Made with ♥ on the Notion Press Platform
www.notionpress.com

Contents

PREFACE

Hi there, this is the mysterious author speaking here. As a child author (yes, I was below 18 when I wrote this book) writing this story was difficult. The book you are about to read is one I did not expect to publish, but here we are. Basically this book was intended to be a fantasy book about dreams but ended up taking a wierd turn towards phycological thriller. Please do enjoy a book I spent way too long trying to publish and write.

Acknowledgements

Sooo, there are a lot of people I would like to thank for their support and inputs,
    ---- Firstly my family friends,

- Arif Vakil, fellow author, Sufi Comics
- Dr Taha Mateen
- Shafaat Shabandari
- Mohammed Iqbal

    ---- My school mate and a close friend for giving his insights,

- Tanmay Nambiar

    ---- And finally my family, without whom I would not have written this book.

I

The Familiar Stranger

The hum of the computer screens was like a dull heartbeat in the dimly lit office. It was well past midnight, but the numbers on the screen blurred together as if they had lost meaning hours ago. Oliver Hale leaned back in his chair, rubbing his eyes until colours swirled behind his eyelids. The room was almost silent except for the steady hum of machines and the occasional creak of the building settling.

Another late night. Another mountain of unfinished work.

Oliver had long since lost track of time. When he first started working at the company, he'd been driven—hungry for success, for recognition. The longer hours he put in, the more praise he'd received from his superiors. But somewhere along the way, the work had consumed him. What started as ambition had become something else, something darker—a compulsion, a need. His life had folded into this office space. The white glow of his monitor was more familiar than sunlight.

A quick glance at the clock showed it was past two in the morning. He wasn't even surprised. It had been like this for years now. The dim overhead lights buzzed, casting long shadows across his desk. Everyone else had left long ago, their desks empty and clean. Yet here he was, hunched over in the silence, surrounded by a mountain of files and unread emails.

He knew he should go home. He should close his laptop, stand up, and leave the building. But there was always *one more thing* to finish. One more task that could make tomorrow easier. One more email to answer. His phone buzzed with a notification, but he didn't check it. Not now. Not when he was so deep into the work that everything else—his personal life, his health, his friends—seemed to fade into the background.

Leaning back, Oliver let his gaze wander toward the window. His office had a view of the city, but it was nothing like the glittering skyline they showed in glossy ads. It was more industrial—a sprawl of grey buildings and dimly lit streets. There was no beauty in it, no romance. Just a city grinding through the night, like him.

He hadn't been out with friends in months. If his phone wasn't on silent, it would likely be filled with unanswered messages, half-hearted invitations that he'd ignored for the sake of work. His friends had learned not to bother anymore. He was "too busy," they'd say. Always too busy. But if he wasn't working, then what was he doing? *What else was there?*

The thought lingered, a bitter taste in the back of his mind. But before he could dwell on it, a sharp pain shot through his temples. Another headache. They had become more frequent lately, no doubt from the lack of sleep. His body was protesting, but he had learned to push through.

He sighed, rubbing his temples, then saved his progress on the document in front of him. *It can wait till tomorrow*, he finally told himself. Standing up, he stretched, his joints stiff from hours of sitting. He grabbed his coat from the back of his chair and headed for the door, the sound of his footsteps echoing in the empty hallways. As he reached the elevator, he caught his reflection in the glass doors—unkempt hair, dark circles under his eyes, and a distant, tired look on his face. He hardly recognized the man staring back at him.

The ride down was silent except for the soft hum of the elevator. As he exited the building and stepped onto the sidewalk, a gust of cold air hit him, sharp and biting. He pulled his coat tighter around himself, glancing up at the sky. The city was eerily quiet, the streets empty. A few flickering streetlights illuminated the roads, casting long shadows across the pavement.

As he walked, his footsteps sounded unusually loud in the stillness. The quiet was unsettling, almost oppressive. The only sound came from the occasional rustling of leaves in the wind. But then, something else caught his attention. Out of the corner of his eye, he saw a figure standing across the street. It was just a glimpse, but it made him stop in his tracks.

There, in the dim glow of a streetlamp, was a man standing still, facing him. He wore a long coat, and his hood was pulled up, hiding his face in shadow. Something about the figure made the hairs on the back of Oliver's neck stand up.

He blinked. When he looked again, the figure was gone. The street was empty. *Just a trick of the light*, he told himself. He shook his head and kept walking, but the feeling lingered—the sense that someone, or something, was watching him.

That night, sleep came quickly, pulling him under like a heavy blanket. But it wasn't the restful sleep he needed. It never was.

The dream came as it always did, vivid and unsettling. Oliver stood in a forest, the trees towering over him like silent sentinels. The air was thick with mist, swirling around his feet. The ground was soft beneath him, covered in pine needles. Moonlight filtered through the branches, casting strange, shifting patterns on the forest floor.

It was quiet, too quiet. No birds, no wind, just the heavy stillness of the woods. And there, in the clearing ahead, stood the figure. Always the same figure, standing with its back to him, unmoving, waiting.

He felt drawn to it, compelled to approach. His feet moved of their own accord, taking him closer, though every instinct screamed at him to stop. The figure's posture was eerily familiar, and as he stepped into the clearing, the figure turned to face him.

He froze. His breath caught in his throat.

It was him.

The face staring back at him was his own, but different. There was something off—something darker in the eyes, something twisted in the features. It was like looking into a broken mirror, where the reflection was warped and distorted. The other Oliver smiled, but there was no warmth in it—only coldness, a mocking, knowing smile.

He opened his mouth to speak, to ask who—or what—this was, but no sound came out. His legs felt like lead, rooted to the spot. The figure stepped closer, raising a hand as if to reach out to him, but before they could touch, everything went black.

He woke with a start, gasping for air. His heart pounded in his chest, his skin slick with sweat. He sat up in bed, trying to steady his breathing, but the remnants of the dream clung to him like fog, thick and heavy.

It wasn't the first time he'd had this dream. It had been happening for weeks, maybe months, always the same. The forest, the figure, the confrontation with... himself.

He couldn't shake the feeling, even as the day wore on. His mind kept drifting back to the dream, to the figure that had looked so much like him but wasn't. It gnawed at him, a sense of unease that he couldn't explain. He tried to focus on his work, but the usual rhythm of productivity wasn't there. Emails went unanswered, reports were left half-finished.

At lunch, he sat in the break room, staring blankly at his sandwich, the sounds of the office buzzing around him. It felt like he was watching his life from a distance, detached from it all. Like he was there, but not really *there*.

And then, just as he was about to leave for home, it happened again. As he walked down the busy street, weaving through the evening crowd, he caught a glimpse of something—or someone. His eyes locked onto a man walking in the opposite direction, his face obscured by a hood.

But there it was again—his face. His *own* face.

In the sea of people, the man vanished just as quickly as he had appeared, but the chill that ran down Oliver's spine lingered long after.

II

Echoes of Reality

The next morning arrived with a heavy haze hanging over Oliver's thoughts. He blinked against the bright light streaming through his window, the familiar shapes of his room coming into focus. Yet everything felt different—as if a layer of dust had settled over his reality, dulling the colours of his life.

He dragged himself out of bed, each movement a reminder of the unsettling dreams that had plagued him. Breakfast was a half-hearted affair; he poured cereal into a bowl but hardly tasted it, his mind still replaying the image of the shadowy figure from the night before. He shook his head, trying to dispel the unsettling memories, but they clung to him like a stubborn fog.

As he stepped into the shower, the water washed over him, a temporary reprieve from the thoughts swirling in his mind. He let the steam rise, enveloping him like a cocoon, but the moment he turned off the tap, reality came rushing back. He was late for work.

The office was a cacophony of ringing phones and clattering keyboards, the familiar rhythm both comforting and suffocating. As he entered, he felt the eyes of his coworkers on him, their whispers falling silent the moment he approached. Oliver forced a smile, but it felt strained—like he was wearing a mask.

"Rough night, Oliver?" Jake, his office mate, asked, leaning back in his chair with a smirk. "You look like you've seen a ghost."

"Just a long night," Oliver replied, forcing a chuckle as he sank into his chair. But even he knew it was more than that. He turned on his computer, letting the screen illuminate his face, its glow somehow both comforting and isolating.

The morning dragged on, filled with mundane tasks and endless emails. But the shadows from his dream haunted him, lurking just beyond the periphery of his consciousness. Every time he thought he had pushed them away, they would resurface, whispering doubts and questions he didn't want to face.

He glanced at the clock. Hours passed without him noticing, yet the day felt endless. The break room beckoned, and he found himself wandering in there, hoping for a distraction. A few coworkers chatted over their coffees, their laughter echoing against the sterile walls.

"Hey, Oliver! You joining us?" asked Maya, a friendly face with bright eyes and a disarming smile.

"Just grabbing some coffee," he said, pouring himself a cup. But as he turned to leave, he caught a glimpse of something out of the corner of his eye—a flash of movement, a figure in a hoodie disappearing around the corner of the hallway.

His heart raced, a jolt of adrenaline coursing through him. He had seen it again. The same figure, the same haunting familiarity. He set down his coffee, the cup rattling against the counter. "Excuse me," he muttered, pushing past his colleagues and heading into the corridor.

The hallway was busy with employees rushing from one meeting to another, but Oliver barely registered them. He scanned the area, searching for the figure he'd seen. His pulse quickened with every passing moment. But it was gone—vanished into the crowd.

Just as he was about to turn back, he caught a glimpse of a reflective surface in the glass of a nearby window. The figure was there again, standing just outside. This time, Oliver was sure of it. He hesitated; his breath caught in his throat. Should he go after it? Should he confront whatever—or whoever—this was?

In an instant, he decided. Without thinking, he stepped outside. The chill of the air hit him as he crossed the threshold, the noise of the office fading behind him. The street was bustling, filled with the sounds of traffic and people going about their day. But his focus was solely on that figure, who seemed to be moving just ahead.

"Hey!" he shouted, his voice cutting through the noise. "Wait!"

The figure turned briefly, and for a split second, their eyes met. Oliver felt a rush of recognition and dread, but before he could close the distance, the figure dashed down an alley, disappearing around the corner.

His legs carried him forward, fuelled by a mix of fear and curiosity. He turned sharply into the alley; the narrow space lined with graffiti-covered walls. It was darker here, the sunlight blocked by the tall buildings surrounding him.

"Stop!" he called out, but the only response was the echo of his own voice. Oliver paused, panting, scanning the alley for any sign of the figure. *Was it just a figment of his imagination?*

Suddenly, he spotted movement—a shadow flitting between the crates stacked haphazardly against the wall. "Who are you?" he demanded, taking a step closer.

As he approached, the figure emerged from the shadows, pulling down the hood. Oliver's breath caught in his throat as the face was revealed. It was him. A darker version, with a familiar yet unsettling smirk that sent chills down his spine.

"Welcome, Oliver," the figure said, voice smooth yet mocking. "I've been waiting for you."

"What do you want?" Oliver managed to stammer, confusion and anger swirling within him.

"Want? Oh, I think you know," the figure replied, stepping closer, mirroring his movements as if they were in sync. "You've been running from yourself for too long."

"I don't know what you're talking about," Oliver shot back, trying to regain control of the situation. But the figure's presence was magnetic, drawing him in, forcing him to confront his own shadows.

"Look around you," the figure gestured, his arm sweeping across the alley, as if unveiling some grand truth. "You're caught in a cycle, Oliver. You choose work over everything else—friends, family, even your own sanity. This is the life you've built, but is it truly what you want?"

"Stop!" Oliver snapped, shaking his head as if to dispel the illusions. "You're not real. You can't be real."

"Oh, but I am," the figure said, leaning closer. "I'm everything you've buried, every choice you regret. I'm the reflection you refuse to see."

A heavy silence fell between them, the weight of the truth hanging in the air. Oliver felt his heart race as he grappled with the words. He wanted to dismiss the figure, to turn away from this confrontation, but he found himself rooted in place.

"Join me, Oliver," the figure urged, a glint of something darker in his eyes. "We can change everything. You can escape this dull existence and embrace your true potential. All it takes is a little courage."

"What are you talking about?" Oliver felt a swell of anger mixed with fear. "I'm not like you!"

"But you are," the figure pressed, his voice dropping to a whisper. "Every choice you make leads you closer to me. You just need to accept it."

Just then, a loud noise erupted from the street, jolting Oliver from the trance. Horns blared, and the sounds of the city rushed back in, washing over him like a tidal wave. He stumbled back, shaking his head as if awakening from a deep sleep. The figure grinned, a knowing look in his eyes.

"Think about it, Oliver. I'll be waiting," he said, before vanishing into the shadows of the alley, leaving Oliver alone and shaken.

Breathing heavily, Oliver turned and fled the alley, the chill of the encounter still lingering in his bones. He stumbled back into the busy street, the noise and chaos of the city enveloping him once again. But inside, everything had shifted.

What did it mean? Who was this dark reflection of himself, and why did it feel like a confrontation he could no longer ignore? The questions tumbled through his mind as he fought to regain his composure.

As Oliver made his way back to the office, the weight of uncertainty pressed down on him. He could feel the eyes of his coworkers on him, could hear their murmurs. But all he could think about was the figure—the promise of something more, and the darkness lurking just beneath the surface of his carefully constructed life.

III

Fractured Reflections

Oliver spent the remainder of the day in a daze, haunted by the encounter in the alley. The sight of his darker self—the mocking grin, the challenge in those familiar yet foreign eyes—echoed in his mind like a haunting refrain. He returned to his desk, but the usual rhythm of clicking keyboards and ringing phones felt distant, muffled by the weight of his thoughts.

Every time he glanced at the clock, time seemed to mock him, dragging on at an agonizing pace. The fluorescent lights flickered overhead, and he rubbed his temples, trying to dispel the fatigue settling in. He was aware of his coworkers talking, laughing, but their voices faded into a background hum, irrelevant to the storm brewing within him.

When lunchtime arrived, Oliver found himself wandering aimlessly through the nearby park, the midday sun warming his skin. He tried to shake off the unease, seeking solace in the rhythmic rustle of leaves and the laughter of children playing nearby. He sat on a bench, taking a moment to breathe and gather his thoughts. But the serenity around him did little to quell the chaos inside.

"Why do I work so hard?" he muttered under his breath, gazing at the ducks paddling in the pond. The question had been nagging at him for weeks, perhaps months. He prided himself on his dedication, but the dark figure in the alley had forced him to confront a nagging truth: was he chasing success or simply running from himself?

As he watched the ducks glide effortlessly across the water, he couldn't help but wonder what it would be like to embrace that simplicity—to let go of the incessant pressure to succeed and just be. The thought flickered in his mind like a candle struggling to stay lit in a storm.

A soft laugh interrupted his musings. He turned to see Maya approaching, a warm smile on her face, her lunch in hand. "Hey, Oliver! Mind if I join you?"

"Of course," he replied, forcing a smile as she settled beside him.

"Long day?" she asked, glancing at him with concern. "You look a bit lost."

"Just... thinking," he said, unsure how much to reveal. "You know how it is."

"Sometimes I think too much about work, and it gets overwhelming," she admitted, tearing a piece from her sandwich. "But it's important to take a step back and breathe. Life's not all about deadlines and projects."

He nodded, grateful for her understanding. Maya had a way of grounding him, reminding him of the world beyond spreadsheets and emails. Yet, the weight of the encounter in the alley loomed large in his mind.

"Do you ever wonder about the choices you didn't make?" he blurted out, the words tumbling from his lips before he could stop them.

"Of course," she replied, tilting her head. "But I try not to dwell on them. Every choice leads us to where we are now. It's about finding joy in the present, right?"

"Yeah," Oliver said, forcing a smile. But deep down, he felt a flicker of doubt. Was he truly living in the present, or was he simply going through the motions?

After lunch, Oliver returned to the office, but the afternoon dragged on in a blur. He struggled to focus on the tasks at hand, his mind a chaotic whirlwind of thoughts. Every notification on his phone seemed to pull him further away from reality, and he found himself staring blankly at the screen.

Then, just as the day began to wind down, an email notification pinged in his inbox. It was from a colleague about an upcoming project meeting—another deadline looming. With a sigh, he opened it, but the words blurred together, leaving him more frustrated than before. He had always excelled at his job, but lately, it felt like a heavy burden, a weight pressing down on him.

As he scrolled through the email, he caught a glimpse of something on the side of the screen—an advertisement for a weekend retreat focused on mindfulness and self-discovery. The image of serene landscapes and people laughing caught his eye. A small voice in the back of his mind whispered, *maybe this is what you need.*

He hesitated for a moment, fingers hovering over the keyboard. The idea of escaping the monotony of his life, of reconnecting with himself, was tempting. But guilt quickly followed—how could he justify taking time off when there were projects to finish and expectations to meet?

But that dark figure's words echoed in his mind: *You're running from yourself.* Oliver clenched his jaw, determination bubbling to the surface. *What if I need to confront who I am, to understand what I truly want?*

With a surge of resolve, he clicked on the link, his heart racing as he filled out the registration form. It felt like a leap into the unknown, but perhaps that was exactly what he needed.

That night, Oliver fell into an uneasy sleep, his mind a whirlpool of anticipation and anxiety. The retreat loomed over him like a beacon of hope, yet the weight of his reality clung to him, a shroud of doubt.

When he closed his eyes, he was once again drawn into the dream world. The familiar landscape awaited him—a swirling mist surrounding him, the air thick with anticipation. But this time, he felt a shift. There was a sense of urgency, as if something important was about to unfold.

He walked through the dreamscape, and just as he began to feel a semblance of peace, he saw him—the shadowy figure, his dark reflection, standing at the edge of a cliff. The figure turned to face Oliver, his expression a mixture of amusement and challenge.

"Welcome back, Oliver," he said, his voice echoing in the stillness. "Are you ready to embrace the truth?"

"What truth?" Oliver shouted, frustration boiling over. "What do you want from me?"

"I want you to see the choices you've made, the life you could have lived," the figure replied, gesturing toward the horizon where the sky bled into colours Oliver had never seen before—vivid shades of violet and gold, swirling together in a mesmerizing dance.

"Why do you keep showing me this?" Oliver asked, stepping closer to the edge, his heart racing. "What does it mean?"

"It means you have the power to change your course," the figure said, a grin spreading across his face. "But first, you must confront your fears. Only then can you find freedom."

With those words hanging in the air, the dreamscape began to tremble, the colours swirling faster, threatening to pull Oliver into a vortex of uncertainty. He felt a rush of panic as the world around him started to dissolve.

"Wait!" he cried out, reaching for the figure. But just as their fingers almost touched, the dream shattered, and he was thrown back into the depths of darkness.

Oliver jolted awake, heart pounding, drenched in sweat. The sun was barely rising outside, casting pale light through his window. He sat up, the remnants of the dream still vivid in his mind, the figure's words echoing in his ears.

He took a deep breath, trying to steady himself. The encounter had felt real, too real to dismiss. The urgency of the moment lingered, igniting a spark of determination within him. He realized that the weekend retreat was not just an escape—it was a chance to confront his fears, to embrace the choices he had avoided for too long.

As he prepared for the day, Oliver felt a shift within himself—a flicker of hope mingled with uncertainty. He couldn't ignore the call of his dreams any longer; it was time to face the reflections he had long kept hidden.

With a new sense of purpose, he stepped into the morning light, ready to embrace whatever came next.

IV

The Echo of
Another World

The sun hung low in the sky as Oliver stepped out of his apartment, its warmth a stark contrast to the chill that lingered in his thoughts. The retreat loomed ahead, a promise of escape from the encroaching shadows that had haunted him since that fateful encounter in the alley. Yet, as he made his way toward the venue, a nagging doubt gnawed at him. Could this really be the answer to the chaos within?

As he arrived at the retreat centre, a sprawling estate nestled among lush trees, he was greeted by a group of cheerful participants. Their laughter echoed through the air, light and carefree, a melody that felt distant to him. Oliver hesitated, standing at the edge of the gathering, feeling like an outsider in a world that seemed so alive. Yet, beneath the façade of joviality, he sensed an undercurrent of apprehension shared by others, a silent acknowledgment of their own struggles.

"Welcome!" a voice boomed, pulling Oliver from his reverie. A tall woman with an inviting smile and bright eyes approached him. "I'm Clara, the facilitator. You must be Oliver. We're glad you're here."

"Thanks," he replied, forcing a smile as he stepped forward. "I'm excited to be part of this."

Clara's gaze held a depth that made Oliver feel seen, as if she could glimpse the layers beneath his surface. "Let's begin with a short introduction," she suggested, gathering everyone in a circle. "Share your name and what brought you here."

One by one, participants spoke up, each sharing fragments of their stories. Some spoke of burnout, others of loss, but all of them sought solace from the burdens they carried. When it was Oliver's turn, he hesitated, the weight of his truth heavy on his tongue.

"I'm Oliver," he started, his voice wavering. "I'm here because... I feel lost. My life has become a routine, and I'm not sure if it's what I truly want anymore." The words hung in the air, raw and vulnerable.

"Thank you for sharing that, Oliver," Clara said gently. "Recognizing your feelings is the first step. This retreat is about exploring those emotions and finding clarity. Let's begin our journey together."

The day unfolded in a series of workshops and activities designed to delve into self-discovery. Each session peeled back layers of Oliver's carefully constructed persona, revealing the fears and regrets he had long buried. As he participated in guided meditations and group discussions, he felt glimpses of the darkness he had encountered in the alley—the figure lurking in the shadows of his mind.

During a breakout session focused on visualization, Clara guided them to close their eyes and picture a place where they felt safe. Oliver tried to envision a serene landscape, but instead, he found himself in the swirling mists of his dreams, the familiar scene materializing before him. The echoes of laughter faded away, replaced by a haunting silence.

"Oliver, what do you see?" Clara's voice broke through the stillness.

"It's... it's a foggy place," he murmured, a shiver coursing through him. "There's a figure standing at the edge of a cliff. I think it's me... but darker."

"Your darker self?" Clara prompted, her tone encouraging. "What does he represent?"

"Choices I've made... paths I didn't take," Oliver confessed, the weight of his words settling heavily on him. "He keeps taunting me, telling me I'm running from myself."

"Embrace that figure," Clara suggested, her voice steady and soothing. "He's a part of you. What does he want to tell you?"

Oliver's heart raced. The last time he confronted that figure, it had been a battle of wills. But now, in this controlled environment, he felt an odd sense of courage. "He wants me to acknowledge my fears," he said, his voice barely above a whisper. "He wants me to stop pretending everything is fine."

"Let that realization wash over you," Clara instructed, guiding him deeper into the meditation. "Imagine stepping closer to him. What happens?"

As he envisioned himself walking toward the figure, the fog began to lift, revealing not just the shadow but the landscapes of his life—the opportunities he had ignored, the relationships he had sacrificed at the altar of work. He could feel the pull of that darker self, the promise of something more profound lurking beneath the surface. The challenge lay not in denying this reflection but in understanding what it represented.

Suddenly, the vision shifted. The figure smiled—an unsettling blend of familiarity and menace. "Are you ready to face what you've avoided?" he asked, his voice a haunting echo of Oliver's own.

"I'm... I'm trying," Oliver stammered, the weight of his past choices pressing heavily on him. "But it's terrifying."

"Only when you confront the darkness can you truly find your light," the figure replied, gesturing toward the horizon where colours began to emerge—rich shades of orange and pink illuminating the sky.

The meditation concluded, and Oliver opened his eyes, a rush of emotions flooding over him. He felt raw but strangely empowered. The connections he had made with the other participants and the guidance from Clara had stirred something within him.

"Are you okay?" Maya's voice broke through his thoughts as she approached him, concern etched on her face.

"Yeah, just... processing everything," he replied, still shaken from the visualization.

"I felt it too," she said softly. "There's something powerful about facing our fears together. It's liberating."

As they sat together, sharing their experiences, Oliver felt a flicker of hope ignite within him. Perhaps this retreat was more than just an escape; it was a gateway to understanding himself and confronting the echoes of his past.

That night, as they gathered around a fire pit under a starlit sky, Oliver couldn't shake the feeling that the dark figure was still watching him from the edges of his consciousness, waiting for their next confrontation. But now, he sensed that he was not alone in this journey. He had allies, companions who understood the struggle of battling one's own shadows.

As the flames crackled and laughter filled the air, Oliver gazed into the fire, contemplating the journey ahead. It was time to delve deeper into the mystery of his dreams, to explore the ties between this world and the one he had glimpsed in the darkness. He could no longer ignore the call to confront his fears; it was time to embrace the echoes of another world.

V

The Mirror's Edge

Oliver awoke with a start, the lingering weight of the dream pressing against his chest like a leaden blanket. As he lay in bed, sunlight filtered through the curtains, painting stripes of light across his room. Yet, despite the warmth, a chill ran down his spine, a reminder of the shadowy figure that had haunted his dreams.

He sat up, running a hand through his hair as he tried to shake off the remnants of sleep. **Today was the day**—the day he would leave behind the shackles of routine and step into the unknown. The weekend retreat loomed ahead like a beacon, promising answers he desperately sought. Yet, beneath the surface, doubt gnawed at him, the familiar sensation of apprehension creeping back in.

"Do I really want to confront all this?" he whispered to himself, the stillness of the morning amplifying his unease.

After a quick breakfast, Oliver found himself driving to the retreat centre, the hum of the engine barely registering as his thoughts spiralled. He recalled the vividness of his dreams, the darkness that had enveloped him, and the figure that mirrored his own despair. **What awaited him in**

the depths of his subconscious?

As he pulled into the retreat's driveway, surrounded by lush greenery and the distant sound of flowing water, a sense of calm washed over him. But just as quickly, a wave of dread returned, each step toward the entrance echoing the uncertainty building within him. **What if the retreat only deepened his confusion?**

Inside, a cozy lobby welcomed him, adorned with soft lighting and earthy tones. A few attendees milled about, exchanging nervous glances and polite smiles. They were all strangers, yet Oliver felt an inexplicable bond with them. Perhaps they, too, were running from something, trying to escape the burdens of their own realities.

"Welcome! I'm Jenna, your guide for the weekend," a woman with an easy smile approached him, her demeanour warm and inviting. "We're so glad you're here. We'll be diving deep into self-exploration and mindfulness over the next few days. Are you ready?"

Oliver forced a smile, though his heart raced. "I think so."

"Good! Let's gather everyone in the main hall for our first session," Jenna said, leading him down a corridor. The air buzzed with a sense of anticipation, yet Oliver's mind was clouded with questions. What was he truly seeking?

The main hall was a spacious room filled with plush cushions and soft mats, designed for comfort and relaxation. As more participants filtered in, Oliver found a spot near the back, observing the diverse group around him. Some wore expressions of hope, while others masked their apprehension beneath forced smiles.

"Welcome, everyone!" Jenna called, her voice cutting through the chatter. "This weekend is about exploring your inner selves, confronting the shadows that lurk within.

Let's start with a grounding exercise."

She guided them through a series of deep breaths, the room gradually filling with the soothing sounds of collective inhalations and exhalations. As Oliver focused on his breath, he felt a flicker of something deeper within him—a whisper of recognition, a hint of understanding.

But just as he began to settle, his thoughts spiralled back to the figure from his dreams. **What was the connection?**

"Now, let's reflect on our intentions for this retreat," Jenna continued, bringing Oliver back to the present. "Think about what you hope to uncover or let go of this weekend."

As she spoke, Oliver felt a surge of urgency rise within him. **He needed to confront the darkness**, to understand the reflection of himself that haunted his dreams. He closed his eyes and focused on his breath, allowing the tumult of his thoughts to settle.

When he finally opened his eyes, he felt ready. "I want to confront my fears," he spoke aloud, surprising even himself. "I want to understand the choices that have led me here."

A murmur of agreement rippled through the group, and Oliver felt the weight of shared experiences wash over him.

The day progressed with various activities designed to foster self-discovery. They shared personal stories in small groups, practiced meditation, and engaged in expressive art sessions. Each activity peeled back layers of his carefully constructed façade, revealing raw emotions that he had buried for far too long.

But amidst the progress, a nagging thought lingered—**the figure**.

Later that evening, Oliver found himself drawn to the retreat's serene garden. The air was cool, and the sound of crickets serenaded the twilight. He wandered along the winding path, lost in thought, until he stumbled upon a small, ornate mirror perched against a tree.

Intrigued, he approached it, the surface glistening under the soft light of the moon. He peered into the glass, and for a brief moment, he saw not just his reflection but a flash of the dark figure—the smirk, the mocking eyes.

"What do you want from me?" he whispered, his voice barely above a breath.

"Everything," the figure's voice echoed back, resonating through the air as if it was woven into the very fabric of the night.

Oliver stepped back, heart pounding. "Why do you keep tormenting me?"

"Torment? Or awaken?" The figure's voice carried a silky smoothness that wrapped around him. "You've ignored the truth for too long, Oliver. It's time to face what you've been running from."

He shivered, the chill of the night creeping in. "I'm not running anymore," he declared, though his voice wavered slightly. "I'm here to confront you."

The figure appeared in the reflection, leaning closer, the smirk deepening. "Then let's dance, shall we?"

Suddenly, the mirror shimmered, and Oliver felt a pull, an irresistible force drawing him closer. He reached out, fingers grazing the cool surface, and a rush of energy surged through him.

"Step through," the figure taunted. "See what lies on the other side."

In that moment, Oliver felt the boundaries of reality blur, the garden fading away as the world around him twisted and shifted. With a final push, he plunged into the mirror, surrendering to the unknown.

What lay beyond was a realm of fractured reflections, a landscape eerily familiar yet disconcertingly different. The colours were muted, and shadows danced in the corners of his vision. **This was the Mirror's Edge**, a place where choices collided and realities converged.

"Welcome, Oliver," the figure's voice echoed, now more resonant, more vibrant. "You've crossed the threshold. Are you ready to face your true self?"

As he steadied himself, Oliver looked around, heart racing. **This was his chance**—to confront the figure, to understand the darkness within, and to finally unravel the tangled web of his own choices.

"Show me," he said, determination hardening his voice.

With a wave of the figure's hand, the landscape shifted, revealing scenes from Oliver's life—moments of joy overshadowed by missed opportunities, laughter mingled with regret. Each scene played out like a ghost, whispering secrets he had long buried.

"Remember this?" the figure taunted, leaning closer. "You chose work over connection, ambition over love. Every choice has led you here, to this moment of reckoning."

Oliver's heart pounded as he watched his life unfold, a blend of emotions swirling within him. "I was just trying to succeed," he replied, though the words felt hollow.

"But at what cost?" the figure pressed, the mocking smile fading into a look of disdain. "You've built walls to protect yourself, but those same walls have kept you imprisoned."

Oliver clenched his fists, anger and frustration bubbling to the surface. "I didn't know any other way!"

"Ah, but that's the truth you've been running from," the figure countered, stepping back to give Oliver space. "Now, you must confront it. Only by acknowledging your choices can you begin to change them."

As Oliver took a deep breath, the weight of realization settled over him. **This was not just about the figure—it was about him, about his choices, and the life he had crafted.**

He met the figure's gaze, his resolve hardening. "I refuse to be defined by my past mistakes. I can change, and I will change."

The figure's expression shifted, a flicker of something resembling admiration crossing his face. "Very well, Oliver. But remember, change requires courage."

With those words, the world around them trembled, the mirror pulsing with energy. Oliver felt a surge of determination wash over him. This was his moment—his chance to reclaim his narrative and confront the shadows that had lingered for too long.

As the mirror began to crack, shards of reality breaking apart around him, Oliver prepared to face whatever came next, knowing that he held the power to rewrite his story.

VI
Fractured Echoes

The world shattered into a kaleidoscope of colours, each fragment swirling with memories—some sweet, others bitter. As the mirror cracked, Oliver felt a surge of energy, like an electric current coursing through his veins. The fragmented pieces of his past encircled him, resonating with the emotions he had long suppressed.

"Welcome to the realm of fractured echoes, Oliver," the figure declared, now fully materialized beside him. "Here, you will confront the pieces of yourself you've hidden away—the truths you've avoided."

Each shard of memory pulsed with its own light, and Oliver felt an inexplicable urge to reach out, to touch the images suspended in mid-air. With a deep breath, he moved closer to the first shard, and the moment he laid a hand upon it, the scene unfolded before him.

He was back in his childhood home, a warm summer day. Laughter echoed in the air as he and his younger sister, Emma, played in the backyard. They chased each other, the sunlight glistening off their joyful faces, a stark contrast to the heaviness he felt now.

"Remember this?" the figure prompted, a hint of nostalgia lacing his voice. "A time of innocence before ambition clouded your vision."

Oliver's heart ached at the sight. "I remember how happy we were," he replied, watching the carefree dance of his younger self. "But life changed so much after that."

"Exactly. You chose to bury this happiness beneath layers of responsibility and work," the figure pointed out, stepping closer. "You turned your back on what truly mattered. Will you let that joy be forgotten?"

Oliver clenched his fists, torn between longing and regret. "I didn't think it was possible to have both. I thought I had to choose."

The scene began to fade, and he felt himself being pulled away from the memory. **"You've always had the choice**, Oliver. But you allowed fear to dictate your path."

As the first memory dissolved, Oliver's surroundings shifted again, and he found himself standing in the bustling office where he spent countless hours buried in spreadsheets and reports. The atmosphere felt stifling, oppressive—a weight that pressed down on him.

"Here we are. Your sanctuary of productivity," the figure mocked, his voice laced with sarcasm. "A place where dreams went to die."

Oliver felt a pang of shame as he watched his older self, hunched over a desk, fingers racing over the keyboard. Colleagues passed by, laughter echoing in the background, yet he remained isolated, lost in a digital world that offered no solace.

"What do you see?" the figure prompted, leaning against a nearby cubicle.

"I see... someone who's lost," Oliver replied, his voice barely a whisper. "I thought I was building a future, but all

I did was create a cage."

"And this cage has become your identity," the figure said, stepping forward. "You clung to success, believing it would fill the void, but it only deepened it."

As the scene shifted again, Oliver found himself standing in front of a bar, the atmosphere buzzing with laughter and the clinking of glasses. This time, he saw himself seated at the bar, surrounded by friends, yet he felt an overwhelming sense of loneliness wash over him.

"Look closer," the figure urged.

Oliver scrutinized the scene, noticing the forced laughter, the masks his friends wore. They were all seeking an escape, much like him. **But beneath the surface, he felt the disconnection, the realization that they were merely filling voids with temporary pleasures.**

"This was supposed to be fun," he murmured, shaking his head. "But it only made things worse."

"You reached for distraction instead of connection," the figure remarked. "You filled your life with noise, drowning out the cries of your heart."

Suddenly, the scene shifted again, this time plunging him into darkness. Shadows loomed all around him, a cacophony of whispers swirling through the air.

"What is this?" Oliver asked, his heart racing.

"This is your fear, Oliver. The fear you've been avoiding all this time," the figure replied, now ominous in the shadows. "Face it!"

As the whispers grew louder, the shadows shifted to reveal haunting visions of failure and disappointment—missed opportunities, broken relationships, and moments of vulnerability that he had chosen to ignore. Each echo resonated with the pain he had long buried.

"No!" he shouted, but the shadows pressed in, threatening to swallow him whole. "I won't let you define me!"

"You can't escape what you refuse to acknowledge," the figure said, its tone piercing through the chaos. "You need to confront your fears to regain control."

In that moment, something inside Oliver ignited. **He had spent too long running, and it was time to fight back.**

"I refuse to be a prisoner of my past!" he declared, and with that, he reached out toward the shadows, channeling his anger and determination. "I will face you!"

With each word, the shadows flickered, and the whispers began to fade. As he stepped deeper into the darkness, he felt a shift within himself, a newfound strength emerging.

"That's it!" the figure encouraged, a note of approval in its voice. "Embrace your power."

The shadows recoiled, and the echoes of his past began to transform, morphing into images of resilience and growth. He saw himself picking up the pieces, learning from failures, and rediscovering connections.

"Yes! This is the path of acceptance," the figure exclaimed, now almost encouraging. "You are more than your mistakes."

As the darkness receded, Oliver felt lighter, the weight of shame lifting from his shoulders. He stepped forward, finally breaking free from the grip of the shadows, emerging into a bright, expansive landscape.

"This is your chance, Oliver," the figure said, now standing beside him in the light. "You've faced your fears and acknowledged your past. Now, what will you do with this knowledge?"

Oliver looked around, feeling the warmth of the sun on his skin and the breeze against his face. He realized this was a new beginning—an opportunity to redefine himself, to forge a life not dictated by fear or regret.

"I will embrace my truth," he said with newfound conviction. "I will seek balance, reconnect with those I love, and prioritize what truly matters."

"And that is your strength," the figure replied, a soft smile breaking through the earlier facade. "But remember, this is only the beginning. The journey ahead will be filled with challenges."

"I know," Oliver said, determination in his voice. "But I'm ready to face them."

With a wave of the figure's hand, the landscape shifted once more, revealing a path lined with vibrant flowers, each bloom a testament to the growth and healing Oliver was now ready to embrace.

As he stepped onto the path, he felt a rush of excitement and hope. **This journey would not be easy, but it was his, and he was prepared to walk it.**

Behind him, the figure began to fade, a lingering reminder of the darkness he had confronted. **"Remember, Oliver,"** it echoed, "You are the master of your choices. Keep moving forward."

And with that, Oliver stepped forward into the light, the echoes of his past fading behind him, leaving only the promise of a brighter tomorrow.

VII

The Road to Reconnection

The vibrant path stretched ahead of Oliver, each step resonating with a newfound sense of purpose. As he walked, the warmth of the sun kissed his skin, illuminating not just the world around him but also the shadows that had once clouded his heart. He could feel a transformation taking place within him, a gradual unraveling of the tightly wound chains of fear and regret that had bound him for so long.

In the distance, he spotted a small gathering of familiar faces—a picnic unfolding beneath the broad canopy of a majestic oak tree. Laughter bubbled up like a gentle stream, beckoning him closer. His heart raced as he recognized the faces of his friends and family, the very people he had distanced himself from in pursuit of a hollow ambition.

"Am I ready for this?" he whispered to himself, hesitation creeping in like a shadow. But then he remembered the figure's words: **You are the master of your**

choices.

With a deep breath, Oliver approached the gathering, each step imbued with determination. As he drew nearer, he noticed Emma seated on a picnic blanket, her laughter ringing out like a melody. It struck him how much he missed moments like this—the simplicity of connection, the joy of being present with those he loved.

"Oliver!" Emma exclaimed, her eyes lighting up as she caught sight of him. "You made it!"

A wave of warmth washed over him as he joined them, a sense of belonging enveloping him. The picnic was a colorful spread of food, laughter, and stories, a tapestry of shared experiences waiting to be woven anew.

"We thought you'd never come!" one of his friends chimed, teasingly. "We were just about to eat your share of the pie!"

Oliver chuckled, a genuine smile breaking across his face. "I wouldn't miss that for the world!"

As they settled in, he felt the ease of camaraderie wash over him like a soothing balm. They shared stories, laughed about inside jokes, and reminisced about times long past. Each moment stitched together the fabric of their friendship, slowly mending the frayed edges that time and distance had worn thin.

But beneath the surface of the laughter, Oliver felt a weight—an understanding that he had missed significant moments, had neglected to nurture the relationships that mattered most. **He had let ambition overshadow connection.**

"What have you been up to?" Emma asked, curiosity lighting her eyes.

Oliver hesitated, his heart racing. He could share the surface-level details—work projects and long hours—but the truth of his recent journey felt monumental. How could he express the awakening he had experienced?

"Honestly, I've been... reevaluating things," he finally said, his voice steady. "I realized I've been missing out on what really matters—like being here with all of you."

The group exchanged glances, sensing the sincerity in his words.

"It's good to have you back," one of his friends said, placing a hand on his shoulder. "We've missed you."

Their support ignited something within him—a flicker of hope that he could rebuild what had been lost. As the day unfolded, he found himself sharing more of his thoughts, opening up about the internal battles he had faced.

"I felt like I was living two lives," he confessed, his gaze steady. "One filled with work and success, and another longing for connection and happiness. I've realized I can't have one without the other."

"That's a big realization," Emma said, her voice soft yet firm. "But it's never too late to change."

"Exactly," Oliver responded, emboldened. "I want to find balance. I want to be present for all of you."

As the sun dipped low on the horizon, casting a golden hue over the picnic, he felt a surge of optimism. They moved from the blanket to a nearby field, playing games and engaging in friendly competitions. **Laughter filled the air, a melody of joy that lifted his spirits higher than he thought possible.**

Later that evening, they gathered around a fire, the crackling flames providing warmth as they settled into a more contemplative mood. The conversation turned deeper, sharing dreams, aspirations, and fears that lingered beneath the surface of everyday life.

"What do you want, Oliver?" one of his friends asked, breaking the silence.

"I want to build something meaningful," Oliver replied, feeling the weight of his words. "I want to create a life that encompasses both my ambitions and the connections that ground me. I want to make an impact, not just in my career but in my relationships."

"That's a powerful vision," Emma said, a proud smile gracing her lips. "And you can absolutely achieve it."

With each word exchanged, Oliver felt the chains of his past slowly unraveling, the bonds of friendship and love reinforcing his resolve. This was what he had longed for—connection, support, and a sense of community.

As the fire flickered, casting shadows that danced around them, he realized he was no longer defined by his past choices. **He was forging a new path, one filled with promise and purpose.**

Days turned into weeks, and with each passing moment, Oliver made deliberate choices to prioritize his relationships. He reached out to old friends, scheduled regular family dinners, and made time for those he cared about.

With every connection he nurtured, he felt a sense of fulfillment blossom within him, like flowers blooming in spring after a long, harsh winter. He started to share his journey, his struggles and victories, inspiring others to do the same.

"It's liberating to be honest," he would tell Emma during their weekly coffee dates. "I never realized how much I had kept bottled up. Now, it feels like a weight has been lifted."

"You're not alone," Emma reassured him, her eyes sparkling with encouragement. "We all struggle with something. It's about how we face those challenges that defines us."

With each coffee date, each game night with friends, and each heartfelt conversation, Oliver felt himself blossoming into the person he had always wanted to be—someone who was not just driven but connected, not just ambitious but aware.

Yet, the journey wasn't without its challenges. There were moments of doubt when the shadows of his past threatened to creep back in, whispering insecurities and fears that had once held him captive.

"What if I fail again?" he would sometimes think, fear coiling tightly in his chest.

But then he would remind himself of the figure in the realm of fractured echoes—the strength he had discovered by confronting his fears. He had faced the darkness and emerged stronger; he could face the future with the same resilience.

In time, he found ways to balance work and relationships, ensuring he dedicated time to both. He carved out moments to pursue his passions, whether it was painting, writing, or simply spending time with loved ones.

One afternoon, as he strolled through the park with Emma, he reflected on how far he had come. **"I used to think success was about climbing the corporate ladder, but now I see it's about the connections we make along the way."**

Emma smiled, her eyes reflecting pride. **"You're on the right path, Oliver. Just remember, it's a journey. Celebrate every step, even the small ones."**

And celebrate he did. Each laugh shared, each connection deepened, each moment spent in the present became a victory, a testament to the growth he had embraced.

As the seasons changed, so did Oliver. With each passing day, he felt lighter, more attuned to the beauty of life unfolding around him. The road ahead was still unknown, but for the first time in a long while, he felt ready to walk it—not alone, but hand in hand with those who mattered most.

VIII

The Mirror of Choices

Life had settled into a comforting rhythm for Oliver, one that embraced the nuances of both ambition and connection. He felt lighter, more fulfilled, as he navigated the delicate dance between personal aspirations and the bonds he cherished. Yet, as he continued to build his life anew, the universe had a way of throwing unexpected challenges his way.

It was a crisp autumn morning when he received an email that would alter the course of his path once more. The subject line read: **"Promotion Opportunity: Head of Innovations Department."**

As he opened the email, excitement surged within him. The role promised not only a significant salary increase but also a chance to lead a team that would be at the forefront of groundbreaking projects. This was everything he had worked for—an opportunity that aligned perfectly with his professional aspirations.

But with that excitement came an unsettling weight in his stomach. The position would demand long hours and travel, perhaps even taking him away from the community he had worked so hard to reconnect with. Oliver leaned back in his chair, staring out the window as leaves fluttered down like golden confetti. **What would it cost him to accept this promotion?**

He spent the rest of the day in a haze, wrestling with his thoughts. The pull of ambition whispered enticing promises of success and recognition, while the echoes of his recent realizations tugged at his heart, reminding him of the importance of balance and connection.

Later that evening, he met Emma at their favorite café, the aroma of freshly brewed coffee enveloping them as they settled into a cozy corner. As he sipped his drink, he could see the spark of curiosity in her eyes.

"You seem distracted," she noted, tilting her head slightly.

Oliver sighed, running a hand through his hair. **"I received a promotion offer today. It's an incredible opportunity, but..."**

"But?" Emma prompted, her interest piqued.

"But it would mean more hours, more travel, and I'm not sure I want to sacrifice the connections I've just begun to rebuild," he admitted, feeling a weight lift as he spoke.

Emma nodded thoughtfully. **"That's a tough position to be in. What do you really want?"**

"I want to succeed, but I don't want to lose myself again. I've finally found a balance, and I'm scared to disrupt that," he confessed.

"Maybe it's not about choosing one over the other," she suggested. **"Consider what you can do to maintain that balance while pursuing your goals."**

Her words resonated deeply, igniting a flicker of hope within him. Could he find a way to pursue this opportunity without losing the connections he had cherished?

As he weighed his options, he sought the counsel of those who mattered most. He reached out to his friends and family, sharing his dilemma and seeking their perspectives. Each conversation illuminated different facets of his decision.

"You've worked so hard for this, Oliver," his mother encouraged. **"But don't forget what makes you happy. If the job demands too much, it might not be worth it."**

His father added, **"Success means different things to different people. Don't let someone else's definition shape your choices."**

With every piece of advice, Oliver felt more empowered to make a decision that honored both his ambitions and his connections. He began to envision a path that embraced both sides of his life, one where he could grow professionally without sacrificing the relationships he valued.

After much reflection, he drafted a plan—an approach to navigate the new role while maintaining his commitment to his friends and family. He would set clear boundaries, ensuring he dedicated time to his loved ones despite the demands of the job. He would delegate tasks, prioritize efficiency, and carve out moments of personal time amidst the chaos.

As he finalized his plan, he felt a surge of confidence. This was not just a job; it was an opportunity to model the very balance he had fought to achieve. He could take on this challenge while nurturing the connections that had brought him so much joy.

When he submitted his acceptance, a wave of relief washed over him. It wasn't just about the job; it was a declaration of his commitment to living a life that honored both ambition and connection.

In the weeks that followed, Oliver transitioned into his new role with a newfound sense of clarity. He immersed himself in the work, embracing the challenges that came with leading a team. Yet, he remained vigilant in his commitment to his personal life. He scheduled regular family dinners, maintained his coffee dates with Emma, and kept his friends close, ensuring they remained a priority in his life.

The autumn days turned into a symphony of experiences—team brainstorming sessions filled with creative energy, late-night conversations with friends, and laughter shared over family meals. Oliver was living the best of both worlds, weaving together the threads of ambition and connection into a beautiful tapestry.

However, the journey was not without its trials. As the demands of his new position intensified, he felt the strain. Late nights at the office bled into weekends filled with work, and he found himself caught in a whirlwind of responsibilities.

One evening, he returned home to find Emma waiting for him. The worry etched on her face mirrored the unease in his heart. **"You've been working a lot lately,"** she said softly, concern lacing her tone. **"Is everything okay?"**

"I'm just... adjusting," he replied, though he felt the truth hanging heavy in the air.

"Oliver, it's okay to ask for help or take a step back," she urged. **"Don't lose sight of what's important."**

Her words struck a chord within him. He had promised himself balance, yet here he was, teetering on the edge once more.

"You're right," he admitted, feeling the weight of realization settle in. **"I need to reassess my priorities."**

The following days were marked by reflection. Oliver took a step back, re-evaluating how he managed his time. He started delegating more tasks at work and setting firm boundaries to protect his personal time. He made it a point to reconnect with his loved ones, reminding himself of the joy that flowed from those relationships.

Gradually, he regained his footing, finding a rhythm that allowed him to thrive in both his professional and personal life. He learned to embrace flexibility, adjusting his approach as needed while remaining committed to his values.

As the holiday season approached, Oliver found himself enveloped in a sense of gratitude. He organized a gathering to celebrate with friends and family, a reminder of the connections that grounded him.

That evening, as they gathered around the table adorned with delicious food and laughter, he felt a profound sense of fulfillment. He looked around at the faces of those he cherished, and for the first time in a long time, he felt truly at home.

"To new beginnings," he raised his glass, his voice steady. **"And to the people who make life meaningful."**

Everyone joined in, their voices rising in unison, a chorus of celebration that echoed the warmth in Oliver's heart.

As the night wore on, filled with stories and laughter, he knew that he had not only embraced his ambition but had also reclaimed the connections that defined him.

And in that moment, as he basked in the joy of their togetherness, Oliver understood—life was not about choosing one path over another but about weaving the threads of ambition and connection into a beautiful tapestry that reflected his true self.

www.ingramcontent.com/pod-product-compliance
Lightning Source LLC
Chambersburg PA
CBHW031245130726
47988CB00008B/3238